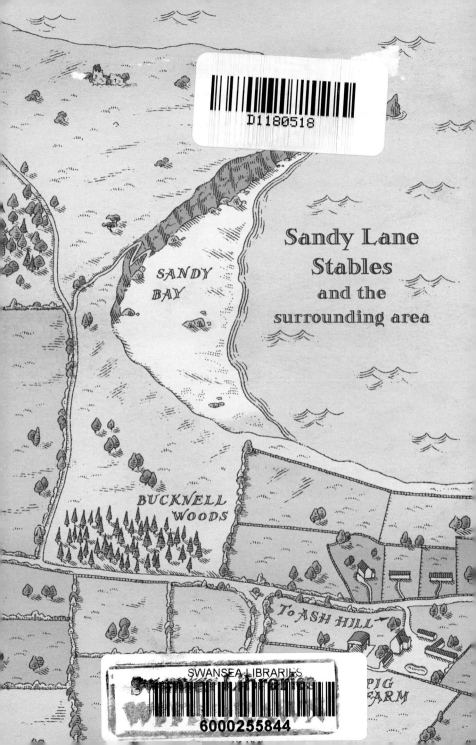

Sandy Lane
Stables
and the
surrounding area

SANDY
BAY

BUCKNELL
WOODS

TO ASH HILL

PIG
FARM

Sandy Lane Stables

Sandy Lane Stables

A Horse
for the Summer

Michelle Bates

Adapted by: Mary Sebag-Montefiore

Reading consultant: Alison Kelly

Series editor: Lesley Sims

Designed by: Brenda Cole

Cover and inside illustrations: Barbara Bongini

Map illustrations: John Woodcock

This edition first published in 2016 by Usborne Publishing Ltd.,
Usborne House, 83-85 Saffron Hill, London EC1N 8RT, England.
www.usborne.com

Copyright © Usborne Publishing, 2016, 2009, 2003, 1996

Illustrations copyright © Usborne Publishing, 2016

The name Usborne and the devices ♀ 🎈 are Trade Marks of
Usborne Publishing Ltd. UKE

A CIP catalogue record for this book is available from the British Library.

Contents

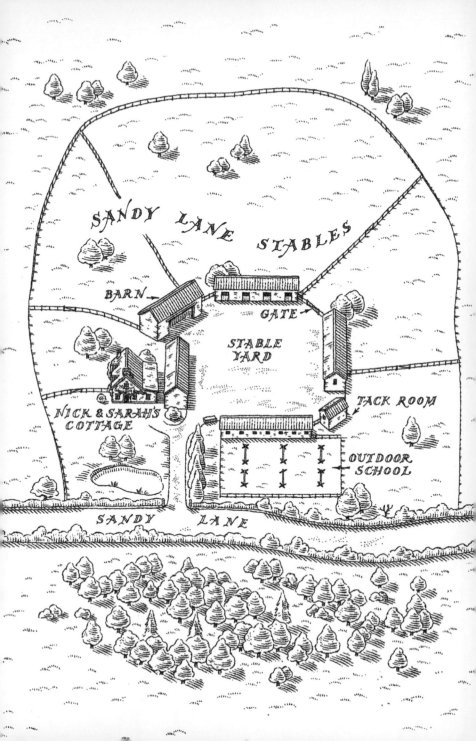

Chapter 1

Exciting News

Tom Buchanan flew into the yard at Sandy Lane Stables. Early morning mist was rising from the ground, filling the air with a hazy glow. He couldn't believe it was two years since he'd started riding there. It seemed as if time had zipped by as fast as he was pedalling his bike. Today had to be the best day so far; he had some amazing news to share. Tom jumped off his bike and charged into the tack room.

"Nick, Sarah, where are you?" he cried, unable to wait any more.

Silence.

Tom called again, louder, but there was still no answer. That was unusual. Nick Brooks and his wife Sarah, the owners of Sandy Lane, were always in the tack room on the dot of eight, planning the day's schedules after the early morning feeds.

Where was everyone? Tom scanned the yard, spying Nick with the vet, coming out of Feather's stable. Tom hoped it wasn't anything serious.

"A sprain in the suspensory ligament... plenty of rest... that's all I can prescribe..."

Tom could hear snippets of the vet's advice.

"Hose her down for the next forty-eight hours to reduce the inflammation, and add a support bandage to the opposite leg. That should help it take the extra weight without becoming too strained."

"So Feather isn't rideable for at least two months." Nick's worried voice echoed around the yard.

Tom groaned. Sandy Lane didn't need an injured horse. Nick and Sarah had bought the stables three years ago, and constantly faced financial difficulties. It was hard enough competing with the established stables in the area – every horse had to be profitable if Sandy Lane was to survive. A horse eating its head off and not working couldn't bring in money, even if the horse was very beautiful. And Feather *was* beautiful. A grey Arab with a ghostly-white coat like a phantom.

Tom knew Feather wasn't really white. Everybody knew a white horse didn't exist. On paper, they were classified as light grey, iron grey, dappled grey or even flea-bitten grey... never white. None of these descriptions quite suited Feather. Flea-bitten was the closest, for the little black hairs over her coat made her look mottled. But Tom didn't think the word 'flea-bitten' accurately described such an awesome horse as Feather.

As Tom gazed across the yard, Feather looked over her door. It was sad to see her confined to the stable. She was one of Nick and Sarah's most valuable and popular animals. There wasn't another horse at the stables like her.

Nick had disappeared again. Everywhere was

quiet this morning. Normally the yard was hustling and bustling by now. Tom guessed Nick must be talking to Sarah at their cottage. He didn't like to disturb them, but felt he'd burst if he didn't tell them his news.

The cottage was just by the stables. Rambling wild roses covered the walls, hiding the crumbling brickwork. It was in dire need of fresh paint. Like everything at Sandy Lane it was slightly shabby.

Both Nick and Sarah rode, though Sarah hardly ever did nowadays. Sorting out the mountain of bills and paperwork that kept flooding in, she was short of time. Nick was always with the horses. He'd been a jockey, but the day his steeplechaser, Golden Fleece, had fallen to her death, he'd vowed never to race again. For ages, Sarah had thought that he'd never even *ride* again. Then they'd bought Sandy Lane and now Nick was trying to put the tragedy behind him.

Tom knocked on the back door. Nick and Sarah were deep in conversation as he walked in, almost tripping over Ebony, the black Labrador, sprawled on the doormat.

"I've been looking for you everywhere," Tom said.

"Uh-oh," said Sarah. "I can't take more bad news."

"It's good news," grinned Tom.

"Tell us," Sarah said gloomily. "It'll make a change from all these bills."

"It's Georgina and Chancey," Tom gabbled. "She's going abroad with her parents and she's left *me* to look after him... to do anything I want with. Isn't it amazing? She'll be away two and a half months... He's mine for all that time. So Horton Chancellor is ready to collect whenever I want."

"Slow down there," said Sarah. "Who are Georgina and Chancey? And *what* is Horton Chancellor?"

"Sorry." Tom blushed. "Georgina is my awful cousin, and Chancey is Horton Chancellor. You remember, the horse that took the showjumping circuit by storm last season when ridden by Emily Manners? My Uncle Bob bought him for Georgina."

"I remember that horse," Nick put in. "A star...

14.2 hands, chestnut gelding, cleared everything in sight. Jumped like a dream."

"That's him," Tom replied. "I've been lent him for the summer and I was wondering... hoping... that I could keep him at Sandy Lane?"

Nick and Sarah looked at each other. This was obviously a chance for Tom, but it might be a disaster for them. With Feather injured, they couldn't afford another horse that wasn't going to earn his keep. But Tom had been indispensable to them for two years. How could they refuse?

Sarah gazed fondly at Tom, remembering the shy eleven year old he'd been when he'd arrived at Sandy Lane. He'd told them then that he'd always wanted to ride, but his parents weren't horsey and couldn't afford it. Then his great aunt had died, leaving the family some money and his parents thought that everyone should benefit. Tom had been given twelve riding lessons and had booked them at Sandy Lane.

After that, Tom was devoted to riding, spending all his spare time at the stables. Nick and Sarah were glad to give him free lessons in return for his help. Tom was to become the first of the group of helpers down at Sandy Lane – the regulars, as Nick and Sarah called them. That made them extra fond of him. And there was no disputing his talent. He was a true horseman, born not made.

Nevertheless, an extra horse meant extra costs and Nick and Sarah had a business to run. Sarah also knew that Tom couldn't afford a livery fee and his mother would never let him keep the horse in her prized garden.

"Stabling a horse isn't cheap, Tom," Nick said thoughtfully.

"I know. But term ends in two weeks, so I'd help out all summer. I'd give you my pocket money. I'd work extra hard..."

"We don't want to be mean," Sarah went on, "but now Feather's injured, we'd have two horses eating and not paying their way."

"Horton Chancellor could pay his way," pleaded Tom. "You could use him in lessons for the more experienced riders instead of Feather. I'd look after him and I could ride him when he's not booked up. He wouldn't be any bother."

"Since you put it like that..." Nick began. Sarah, smiling, raised her eyes to heaven. Tom, waiting for Nick's final words, knew he'd won.

"OK. Bring Chancey to Sandy Lane and we'll see."

Tom was almost stunned with delight. "Thank you, oh thank you! We won't let you down, I promise. Wait till I tell the others."

Chapter 2

Sandy Lane Friends

The others had been as excited as Tom when they heard his news. Alex, Kate, Jess and Rosie were the regulars at Sandy Lane. Of varying riding abilities, they all shared a passion for riding and a love of horses. In the week before Chancey's arrival, they talked of little else but the prize-winning horse.

Tom couldn't stop dreaming of the perfect days ahead. There would be a long summer filled with endless riding days. Tom told himself he'd work hard to become good enough to ride at Benbridge in August – the show that everyone had set their hearts on. He could just imagine it... the breeze whipping past him as he flew around the course and rode through the finish to the sound of thunderous applause...

"That was Tom Buchanan on Horton Chancellor, jumping clear with no time faults..."

Thud! Tom's vision faded as Napoleon kicked over his water bucket.

"Look what you've done!" Tom said crossly, as water flooded the floor of the stable.

Automatically, he started to mop it up, his mind still buzzing with excitement. If someone had told him a month ago he'd be lent a horse for the summer, he would have laughed. Now Chancey was actually arriving tomorrow.

Walking across the yard, Tom refilled Napoleon's water bucket from the old trough. From where he was standing, he could see Rosie and Jess in the outdoor school.

"Heels down, toes in, look straight ahead of you. What's happened to you?" Nick bellowed at them.

"Your hands and forearms should form a straight line with the reins. No point in being here, Jess, if you're not going to concentrate."

Rosie and Jess were in the same year at school – best friends and complete opposites. Where Rosie was careful, quiet and rational, Jess was impulsive, daring and often in trouble.

Their lesson over, the two friends wandered into the yard. Chattering loudly, they tethered their ponies to the rails and set about sponging them down, splashing each other as they worked.

Tom walked to the tack room, smiling to himself. He was small for his thirteen years with untidy brown hair and a round, cheerful face. As the star pupil at Sandy Lane, he could have been arrogant and impossible, yet he wasn't. Always willing to help with whatever needed to be done, Tom was well-liked. There was no horse he couldn't handle, or so Jess and Rosie thought. They secretly admired him and hoped that one day they'd be as good as him.

"Jess, can you tack up Napoleon?" Tom called.

"I have to get Hector ready, and then Nick wants to take the 4 o'clock class."

"Sure," said Jess. "Rosie, could you keep an eye on Minstrel for me?"

Quickly, Jess went into Napoleon's box. Slipping the head collar down his bay neck, she put the bridle on. She was speedy at tacking up now, after a battle learning the basics. Now, without hesitation, she slid the saddle smoothly down Napoleon's back and tightened the girth. Heading out into the blazing sunshine, she took him to the mounting block as Tom led out Hector.

Hector was a big sturdy bay hack, with a coat of polished mahogany. He was Alex's favourite but everyone was fond of him. He was aged twenty, which was old in horse years, but he was a solid ride and ideal for beginners. He was the first horse that Tom had ever ridden. At 16.2 hands, Tom had felt like a sparrow astride an elephant!

Soon everyone was mounted, ready for the ride. Nick looked tired, Tom thought, as he led the group from the yard. He hoped that Nick and Sarah would have more luck this year. Sandy Lane was such a great stables. It seemed wrong that they were continually struggling.

"Tom!" came an excited shout, as the last two of his friends arrived.

"Hi! Alex, Kate, here at last," he yelled. Alex and Kate were brother and sister and usually went everywhere together.

"We had to go to Aunt Claire's fortieth birthday party," groaned Alex. "A nightmare. Everyone telling us how much we'd grown. We got here as fast as we could. No more family gatherings till Christmas, I hope. What's the news on Chancey?"

"He's arriving tomorrow at eleven," Tom said, looking around at his friends. "Can you all be here?"

"Sure," everyone chorused. "Couldn't miss it."

"Alex, could you help me keep busy?" asked Tom. "Turn out the horses with me? If I'm not active every minute until I go to bed, I know I'll be too excited to sleep tonight."

Chapter 3

A Bad Beginning

The next morning, Tom woke early. Too early. By seven, he was in his jodhpurs, gazing out of the window. He smiled. It was going to be a sunny day.

Tom raced downstairs, escaping his mother's breakfast call, speeding as fast as he could on his bike to Sandy Lane.

Not far now. Out of breath, he zoomed up the driveway and hurtled into the yard. The stables were already buzzing with activity.

"Throw me a dandy brush, Tom," Jess called. She was grooming Minstrel, a skewbald, so the white parts of him showed up really muddy. Tom handed her the dandy brush and made a start on Napoleon as they chatted away.

By eleven, Nick had taken two classes and a hack. As usual, Alex and Kate were late and didn't get to the stables until five past, when most of the work was done. Then came the moment everyone had been waiting for. A horse box juddered to a halt beside them. Chancey had arrived.

A disgruntled-looking man stepped out, alone.

Where's Georgina? Tom thought. *Why hasn't she come to settle Chancey in and say goodbye?*

"Hey, you've got a raving monster there," said the man, hunching his shoulders. "I only just managed to get him in the box, and the journey was something else. I thought he'd kick the box down." Before Tom could reply, he'd driven away, fast.

With a frantic whinny and drumming hooves, Chancey pranced down the ramp. He didn't look anything like the sleek, well turned-out horse Tom remembered last season. He was still unclipped and his shabby winter coat was flecked with foam as he pawed the ground feverishly. No one knew quite what to say.

"Is it the same horse?" Rosie piped up.

"He'll look fine once he's clipped," Tom snapped.

"Really?" Jess muttered.

"Shouldn't he be clipped already?" said Rosie. She'd read in her Pony Club manual that horses should be clipped before January, or their summer coat would be spoiled.

"Maybe, but it's not a problem," said Nick kindly. "Take him to his new home, Tom."

Tom approached the horse with the head collar but Chancey jumped skittishly from side to side, rolling his eyes and flicking his tail as Tom led him away.

Tom was confused. Last season, Chancey had been one hundred percent fit, his muscles rippling under his glossy chestnut coat. Still, Tom was sure he was the same horse.

He picked up the things the driver had dumped

in the yard. A saddle and bridle, an expensive-looking rug and a box of smart grooming brushes that looked like they'd never been used. Then he grabbed an old body brush and curry comb, and hurried back to Chancey's stable, opening the door slowly, so as not to startle him.

"Let's get you cleaned up for lunch. I bet you're hungry," he crooned.

Chancey nuzzled Tom's pockets inquisitively. Tom fumbled around for a mint. The horse's lips were as soft as crushed velvet as he accepted it.

"That's better," said Tom. "We need to be friends if we're spending the whole summer together."

The nuzzling turned into frantic chewing.

"Hey, stop!" said Tom. "My jacket doesn't taste that great!" Gently, he pushed Chancey's nose away.

"I've got to go home for lunch," Tom went on, giving him a quick rubdown. "I'll be straight back. Nick says we can join the 3 o'clock class, Chancey."

Chancey's head was buried deep in bucket of pony nuts. He wasn't interested.

Tom's mother insisted upon a family lunch and he tried to get home for it as often as he could, if only to stop her from constantly complaining about all the time he spent at Sandy Lane.

He raced back, to find his family at the table.

"So, how was Georgina?" asked Tom's dad. "Did you thank her for lending her horse?"

"She didn't come," said Tom. "Weird."

"Not necessarily," said his mother. "Maybe she was busy packing before she went away. It always takes me ages to pack."

Tom shrugged. He wasn't convinced. He knew he would always have found time to say goodbye if he'd been lucky enough to own a horse.

"What's Chancey like?" asked his dad.

"OK," said Tom.

"He must be better than OK," said his mother. "You've been so excited…"

"I haven't tried him yet," Tom said tiredly. He didn't want to tell them how wild Chancey had looked. They'd only worry. As soon as lunch was over, he biked back to Sandy Lane and went in search of Nick.

He didn't have to look far. Nick was sitting at the desk in the tack room, signing people in for the next ride and collecting the money.

"Who's in the 3 o'clock, Nick?" Tom asked.

"Anna, Mark, Claudine, Lydia and... someone I don't remember... Who was it now? Oh, could it be you?" Nick smiled teasingly.

"Wow!" Tom gasped. These were good riders. He hoped he wouldn't let Chancey down.

"Ready to tack up Chancey, Tom? We're almost ready to start."

"Sure," Tom smiled, hurrying off.

As he let himself into the stable, Chancey's brown face turned to look at him enquiringly. Tom patted his neck and tickled his nose, letting the horse smell his clothes to get used to him. Then, deftly, he tacked him up and led him out of his stable, into the outdoor school. Rosie, Jess, Alex and Kate were watching.

"He looks much better now he's been groomed and rested," said Rosie.

"And he's lost that mad glint in his eye," added Jess. "The journey probably unsettled him."

Tom felt proud as he walked around the school. He knew he was on a good horse and trembled with anticipation at the power beneath him. Chancey arched his neck and let out a whinny. He was well proportioned, with shoulders that sloped smoothly up to his withers and wide, muscular flanks.

Loosening up their horses, the riders started at a rising trot and then, one by one, began to canter around the track. Chancey wanted to take the lead and Tom had a hard time keeping him behind the others.

"Return to the walk and shorten your stirrups, please. We'll try some jumping," Nick called, sending everybody to the other end of the outdoor school.

They were starting with a pair of cross poles and jump from the trot. Anna trotted Hector round, popping him neatly over the jump, as did the other riders. Tom felt uneasy as Chancey jogged on the spot, fighting for his head.

Looking back, Tom couldn't remember when everything began to go wrong. Chancey had already started shying at imaginary shadows and Tom was finding it difficult to hold him. As the pair approached the jump, Chancey threw his head in the air and dashed towards it.

"Try not to check him too much, Tom," Nick shouted. "He's fighting you for control. If you alter his strides, he'll lose his balance."

With a loud snort and a flash of his tail, Chancey ducked out from the jump and swerved to the right. Then he was off, charging round the paddock. Three circuits later, an ashen-faced Tom had managed to stop him.

"Right Tom," Nick called. "That's enough excitement for one day."

"That horse looks crazy," said Anna. "He's not at all like Feather."

Secretly Tom agreed. And he knew that Chancey

was meant to be a replacement for Feather.

"Tom, don't worry," said Nick, seeing the despair on Tom's face. "We'll talk later."

Back in Chancey's stall, Tom started to untack him, with a sigh.

"Why did you make me look like that?" he asked. "You totally humiliated me. No one will want to ride you now. What will Nick and Sarah do?"

Chancey stared back balefully.

"I'm not going to let you win," Tom declared. "I know how good you were once. I'm going to make you as good as that again. I swear it."

Chapter 4

Back to Square One

Tom got home late, pushed open the door and slunk upstairs. His mother saw he was upset and didn't stop him.

Alone in his room, Tom lay on his bed and sighed. Doubts surged round his mind. Every wall in his room was covered with posters of horses and famous riders. He'd always dreamed he could be as good as them. How silly he'd been. He was hopeless. Today had proved it.

"It was my fault, not Chancey's," he said aloud. "If I'd been at all capable, I could have controlled him."

He put his head in his hands. Clearly the horse wasn't lesson material and Nick and Sarah couldn't keep Chancey at Sandy Lane for free.

At the same time, Nick and Sarah were saying the same thing in the cottage.

"We must be realistic. We can't use him. Suppose he went crazy with one of our clients? It would ruin our reputation," said Sarah.

"You're right," Nick said glumly.

"We should buy another horse to replace Feather. You must simply tell Tom we can't keep Chancey," she declared.

"We can't do that, Sarah. You know Tom's set his heart on having him."

"But we agreed on the understanding that we'd use the horse in lessons," said Sarah, "and that's now impossible. We can't support *two* horses that aren't working."

Nick looked downcast. "Chancey is a magnificent animal. If we can get him back to his old self, we could use him. And if he performs well at shows, it'll enhance Sandy Lane's reputation."

"And if we can't?" Sarah was voicing Nick's worst fears. "He's been ruined, somehow."

"We could sell Whispering Silver," Nick said tentatively. "We'd get a good price for her. She'd make a great hunter and then we could afford to buy a replacement for Feather and have some money left over to buy another horse too."

Sarah smiled at him fondly. He really meant it; giving up the horse he valued most in the world – Whispering Silver, the retired racehorse he'd nursed back to health. No one had believed Nick could do it. Sarah remembered the day he'd bought her at the sale, saving her from the knacker's yard. In the end it had turned out all right, but for a while her life had hung by a thread.

"Oh, Nick, you can't. She's yours. She couldn't belong to anyone else. You saved her life." Sarah took a deep breath. "We'll find the extra money somehow. If we study the horse magazines we'll get something, though we can't aim as high as Feather."

"Horses are much more expensive if you buy them privately. Couldn't we..."

"No more public auctions," groaned Sarah. "It's too risky. You don't know what you're buying. We want guarantees, vets' certificates…"

"I know you're right, really," said Nick.

"Will you tell Tom?" she asked quietly.

"I'll do it now."

Sarah looked at her watch. "It's very late to turn up uninvited."

"I know. But he was so disappointed; I don't want to phone or text. I need to see him."

"OK," said Sarah. "And sort out a training programme…?" she said, with a smile.

Nick hurried out of the cottage, climbed into their old Land Rover and headed for Tom's house. It was in an estate of similar houses, all with paved paths, well-kept flower beds, stripy mown grass and clipped hedges. Nick couldn't imagine Tom being allowed in the kitchen in his dirty riding boots.

Mrs. Buchanan was surprised to see Nick at the

door, but asked no questions. "He's upset about something," she said. "I hope you can help." She turned to the stairs. "Tom, you have a visitor."

Tom came down slowly. He knew why Nick had come. After all, he and Sarah had a business to run.

"You don't have to explain. I know Chancey's hopeless." Tom blurted out the words.

"Wait," said Nick looking surprised. "I didn't come here to say that. Yes, things went wrong this afternoon. But Chancey was and could still be a champion. We can't use him in lessons right now, so Sarah and I will buy a horse to replace Feather..."

"I'm sorry, Nick," Tom interrupted.

"Wait," said Nick again. "That's not your problem. It's ours."

Tom was listening desperately.

"Sarah and I have decided to take a chance with Chancey, if you'll excuse the pun," smiled Nick. "Work hard and you can keep him at Sandy Lane."

"I will," Tom nodded, hardly able to believe it.

"Right. We'll have to take him back to the

beginning and school him again. I don't want to guess what your cousin did to him. But I know Chancey was once a champion, and he can be again. We've got just under eight weeks if he's to be ready for the Benbridge show at the end of August. Do you want to take on the challenge?"

"Sure," said Tom, grinning with relief. "What can I do?"

"First, he must be clipped. I'll organize that this week while you're at school. And he'll need to be shod and have his teeth checked. They'll probably have to be rasped. Then we must discuss a schedule for training and fitness, and carefully monitor his eating habits."

"I can do that," said Tom, eagerly.

"I haven't time to help you straight away. Sandy Lane is busy right now, so you must be patient," Nick continued. "Most important of all, Tom, you must promise you won't take Chancey out on your own. We can't trust him. He's dangerous. Sarah would never forgive me if you got hurt. Besides, I don't want people thinking we're not safe at Sandy Lane. So, do I have your word?"

"Of course, Nick. I promise."

"Fine. Come down to the stables after school on Wednesday. I should have done some work with him by then. I've got a spare hour at five. We could spend it in the outdoor school."

"Great!" Tom beamed.

Everything had been decided so quickly. Tom looked at Nick, half-embarrassed.

"Will you thank Sarah for me? And... thank you Nick."

Nick smiled as Tom showed him out.

Time seemed to pass slowly until Wednesday. When the school bell rang at the end of the last lesson, Tom was the first to get to the classroom door and first to race out of the building.

At last he got to Sandy Lane, hurrying straight to the outdoor school. There was Nick with Chancey on a lunge rein. The saddle on Chancey's back looked strange without any stirrups. As he trotted around the school, he looked like a different horse. He was calm for a start.

"I've been lungeing him since Monday. He's been improving daily. Come into the middle here," said Nick, clicking Chancey on into a canter, flicking the whip lightly towards his hock. "He hasn't forgotten his paces."

Nick slowed Chancey down to a trot with the word 'ter-rot'. Tom walked into the school and took the lunge rein that Nick offered him. Nick stood next to Tom and guided him through the horse's paces. Tom only needed to use the whip lightly as Chancey began to respond to the sound of his voice.

"Very good," said Nick. "Let's try him with some loose jumping. I think Georgina must have been fighting with him for control before a jump. That's why he's so nervy. Every horse likes to find his own natural take-off point." Nick put up some cross poles and got Tom to lunge Chancey over them.

"You see. He jumps perfectly on his own. And because the poles are crossed, it gets him to take off in the middle of the jump. Give him another five minutes and then we'll put him away for the night," said Nick. "He's been so well-behaved. We don't want to push him too hard. We could try riding him out at the weekend. It's just a matter of building up trust. He's not really a problem horse and he's not too old to learn..." Nick's voice tailed off as his mobile rang.

"Speak to you later, Tom," said Nick, attending to his call.

"You see, there's hope for you yet," Tom said, turning to lead Chancey up the drive, crunching across the gravel. He led the horse to his box and gave him a quick rub down. Tenderly, he pulled Chancey's ears before bolting him in for the night. Slinging the bridle over his shoulder and carrying the saddle on his arm, he crossed the yard to return them to the tack room.

"I'm going to the Ash Hill horse sale on Saturday morning, Tom," Nick called. "Why don't you come with me? We can look around."

"But Sarah always says it's too risky to buy at an auction," Tom called back, confused. Nick didn't reply; he was out of earshot. Tom shrugged. He was pleased that out of everyone, Nick had asked him to go. But he was also disappointed; he'd really hoped to ride Chancey on Saturday morning.

Tom headed off on his bike into the still evening. At long last he felt that he was getting somewhere with Chancey. The day had been a turning point for them both.

Chapter 5

Storm Cloud

Saturday! Tom looked out of the window and smiled. He'd be able to spend the whole day with Chancey. Then he groaned... the Ash Hill sale, and Nick had asked him to go. He'd have to hurry; it started at nine. Hurriedly, he threw on some clothes, grabbed a slice of bread and rushed out to his bike.

Nick was already waiting when Tom reached the yard. "OK, Tom?" he smiled. "We'll only look at the horses that are fully warranted. I want to see what's around right now, but we're not buying anything."

"Should we take the horse box – just in case?"

"No," Nick said, rather too quickly. "Then we won't be tempted."

Tom smiled. He knew if Nick got carried away, nothing would stop him from being tempted.

They jolted in the Land Rover out of Sandy Lane towards Ash Hill. It didn't take long to get there.

Tom found Ash Hill really depressing. He frowned, staring in despair at the long rows of horses. All these horses and ponies – creatures from good homes and once well-loved – now stood alone awaiting their fate.

"Look at this one in the catalogue," said Nick.

"Registered yellow Dun working pony, rising four, two white socks, 13.2 hands without shoes. Fully warranted. Sounds good," Tom read.

"Shall we go and check him out?"

But they didn't get that far. As they strolled down the lines of horses, Tom saw Nick's gaze light upon a fragile, dappled-grey pony in the corner. Tied to a muddy piece of rope, her head downcast, she didn't even look up as they approached. And she was so thin. Gently, Nick stroked her shoulder as she tilted her delicately dished face towards him, nuzzling his pockets for titbits. Quickly, he ran his hands down her legs. Tom knew from that moment that Nick was caught.

"There isn't time to see her run up in hand. Look at the welts in her coat, Tom. She's been badly neglected, but her general stance is good. Quick! The bidding's starting."

They hurried to the ringside, and Nick opened his catalogue.

"Lot number one. Who'll start me at seven hundred for this bay cob?" the auctioneer was saying. "Seven hundred. Am I bid seven fifty? Seven fifty, I'm bid. Eight hundred?"

It was happening so rapidly, that Tom could hardly keep up. In seconds, the cob was sold to a man at the back.

"Knackers," said Nick. Tom blinked away the tears welling up in his eyes. He wished he was tougher. If only he were rich, he'd buy them all.

"Ten more lots until ours," Nick whispered.

As the little grey pony was led around the ring, the auctioneer called, "Four hundred?" Nick raised his card in the air.

There was a deathly hush. Tom took a deep breath, praying no one else would bid.

"Any advance on four hundred? Who'll give me four fifty? All done at four hundred?"

Tom held his breath.

"Four hundred I'm bid once. Four hundred twice. Going... going... gone."

The auctioneer banged his hammer on the desk.

"Sold," he said, staring straight at Nick. Tom and Nick exchanged a grin. They had got her.

"Name?" he called.

"Nick Brooks," Nick answered.

"Address?" the man returned.

"Sandy Lane Stables, Colcott."

It was all over, and the auctioneer was dealing with the next lot.

Once they had paid and collected the relevant

papers, Tom and Nick made their way to the little grey pony. Nick untethered her, talking to her all the time in a soft voice.

"We'll soon have you home," he soothed her.

"What's she called?" Tom asked quietly.

"Storm Cloud," Nick answered.

"Perfect," Tom breathed, as the three of them walked slowly away from the sale.

"Why don't you ride her and I'll lead," Nick suggested. "We can come back later to pick up the Land Rover."

"OK," said Tom, bending his knee for Nick to give him a leg-up. "What's Sarah going to say?"

"She won't be pleased at first, but when she sees Storm Cloud she'll feel differently. Sarah pretends to be as hard as nails, but she's really a bit of a softie."

"At least Storm Cloud's fully warranted," said Tom. "So you shouldn't have to pay any vet's bills. Fingers crossed."

Slowly, they picked their way along the grass verge by the roadside, as the traffic sped past. Storm

Cloud didn't even flinch at the cars.

"She has a nice long stride," Tom continued. "She just seems a bit tired."

"She needs feeding up," said Nick. "There's plenty of summer grass for her to tuck into at home."

"Could we do some training with Chancey this afternoon, Nick?" Tom asked.

"Sure. Sarah's taking out the hacks," he replied. "It'll be a good opportunity to get started with him."

"Great," said Tom.

In no time they were back at Sandy Lane.

"Tom, could you sort out Storm Cloud for me?" said Nick. "Put her in the loose box by the tack room. I'll tell Sarah about our latest acquisition," he added sheepishly.

"OK," said Tom, jumping swiftly to the ground. "Come on, Stormy," he whispered, as he led her to the stable. She was sweating slightly, tired after the long walk home. Tom rubbed her shivering body with a wisp of straw.

Moments later, Nick appeared with Sarah. Tom

led Storm Cloud out and circled her as a group gathered to see the latest addition, waiting to hear if she was given the Sandy Lane seal of approval. Quickly, Sarah ran her hands down the horse's legs.

"She's sound, and she has kind eyes, even if she doesn't look in great shape." She patted her on the shoulder. "She'll soon fill out," she smiled, turning to Nick, "even if she was from a sale." Everyone breathed a sigh of relief. Sarah was knowledgeable and her verdict was positive.

Tom hurried off to prepare a quick bran mash for Storm Cloud. It didn't take him long to get her rugged up and give her a quick rub down. And then he raced to get Chancey ready. Feeling guilty that his beloved horse had taken a back seat, so enthralled had he been with the dappled grey pony, Tom determined to make an extra good job of grooming him. He worked until he almost saw his reflection in Chancey's coat. Putting the bit into the horse's mouth, Tom slipped the bridle on and did up the throat lash. Carefully, he slid the saddle down

Chancey's back and tightened the girth. Adjusting his riding hat, he led the horse out of his stable.

"Wow!" said Nick. "You've done an amazing job. Chancey looks wonderful."

"Do you think he's really ready to ride?" Tom stammered nervously.

"He'll be OK if we take it slowly," said Nick.

Climbing into their saddles, they strolled out of the yard and through the gate at the back. Tom hummed happily as they lengthened their reins and rode across the fields. It was a beautiful July day; the aquamarine sky was intense and the smell of the country engulfed them. Chancey's coat shone a burnished red as the sun beat down on their backs. Tom didn't think he'd ever feel happier, as he lost himself in his riding.

Soon, they were crossing the old coastal track over to the open fields that led to the cliff tops. Tom could smell salt in the air. Chancey snorted excitedly, swishing his tail with a determined air.

"Let's canter," Nick suggested. "Stay behind me

and try to let me go for a few strides before you let Chancey follow on. I don't want you forcing me into a gallop. Luckily Whisp is too old to panic, so she'll hold you back."

Tom crouched low in the saddle, urging Chancey on. They rode like the wind and, as they pounded across the springy turf, it seemed as though they were covering miles. All at once, a fallen tree blocked their path. For a moment, Tom was startled. What would Chancey do? Then he remembered Nick's teaching – let the horse do the work and don't interfere. Scornfully, Chancey soared three feet above the log.

"That was magnificent Tom," Nick said, amazed. "He jumps like a stag. I haven't seen a horse like him in a long time."

Tom smiled as they slowly ambled back the way they'd come. Winding through the little copse of trees, they let their horses stretch their heads after their exertions. Finally, they were at the gate to Sandy Lane and clattered happily into the yard.

Chapter 6

Tom's Secret

It was a wet, muggy morning. Tom watched the rain splatter down the tack room's window pane, feeling fed up. He hadn't ridden Chancey for over a week.

Pitter... patter... pitter... patter. The summer rain hammered rhythmically against the glass. In the condensation, Tom traced the horse's head that he had become so good at drawing.

Nick hurried in out of the rain, holding his anorak over his head as an umbrella.

"I've been lungeing Storm Cloud. She has real

potential. If she continues that way I'll be soon be able to use her in lessons," Nick said proudly. "What's up?" he asked, seeing Tom's glum face.

"Nothing really. I was just wondering if you'd have time to look at Chancey and me today?"

"Sorry, Tom. I haven't a spare moment," Nick answered. "I've got two classes, maybe three and then I really need to do another hour with Storm Cloud. You could lead him around the school for half an hour if you like."

"Could I ride Chancey in the hack?" Tom pleaded.

"Not a good idea, Tom. He's not ready. You know how agitated he gets if he's with more than one horse. He tried to kick Jester last time he was out."

Tom sighed impatiently. He knew what Nick was saying was true, but at this rate, Chancey was never going to be ready for the Benbridge show. He felt mean complaining. Nick and Sarah had done everything for him. If it wasn't for them, he wouldn't even have had a home for the horse. Nevertheless, Chancey did need to be schooled if he was going to get fit. And if Nick didn't have time, there was nothing Tom could do about it... Or was there?

And suddenly it came to him. Perhaps *he* could train Chancey. Nick didn't need to know. Chancey had gone really well for him last time he had ridden him and he hadn't really needed Nick there, had he?

Tom sighed again. He knew it wasn't totally true. He did need Nick, and Nick had expressly forbidden him to take Chancey out on his own.

Tom stepped outside. It was spitting as he crossed the yard to Chancey's stable.

"If I got up really early and trained you, nobody would notice," Tom whispered, trying to convince himself that he'd be doing nothing wrong. "You'd like that too, wouldn't you boy?" he murmured. "You'd get out more. We'd have to be very careful that we weren't caught, that's all."

Chancey snorted, as if in response, a piece of straw hanging from his mouth.

"You shouldn't be chewing on that," said Tom crossly. "If you eat too much straw, you'll get colic."

That was what made Tom's mind up. If Chancey was eating his bed, he must be bored.

"We'll start training tomorrow. I'll get here early to tack you up."

"What are you doing in there, Tom?" asked Alex, poking his head over the stable door and grinning. "Talking to yourself?"

"No," said Tom, reddening. "To Chancey."

"You're crazy!" Alex chuckled. "What are you telling him?"

The thought of confiding in Alex passed fleetingly through Tom's mind. It wouldn't be fair, he decided. He couldn't expect Alex to lie for him. He had to bear the full responsibility himself.

"So, are you going out on the 12 o'clock hack? Tom? *Tom?*"

Tom realized that Alex had called his name twice. "N-No," he stuttered. "I'm off home. Will you say goodbye to the others for me?"

"Sure," said Alex, puzzled. It was unlike Tom to spend any time away from Sandy Lane.

Tom wanted the afternoon to think about how he could put his plan into action. He also couldn't bear the thought of being around Nick and having to lie to him. Once he had started the training and Chancey had started to improve, it would all seem worth it.

Back home, Tom, feeling like a criminal, grabbed a notebook and pencil. "Nick brings the other horses in from the fields at seven thirty," he muttered to himself, "so we must start at six to finish in time."

He wrote it all down in a timetable. He'd have to be at the stables at five thirty. Tom groaned. It was a very early start. How long would he have to do that for? And what about a training programme? Tom pondered and planned for the rest of the day.

His alarm went off at five fifteen the next morning. He rubbed his eyes and quickly switched it off. Pulling on his jodhpurs, he tip-toed downstairs and out of the sleepy house. His heart was beating fast and there was a knot in his stomach. There would be real trouble if he was caught.

Nothing stirred, nothing rustled, as Tom cycled along to the yard. The stables were silent, unnervingly still and quiet as he crept to Chancey's stable.

"Sshh," said Tom, stifling Chancey's whinny with a sugar lump as he tacked him up. Nick would surely hear the clatter of Chancey's shoes on the gravel as he was led out of his stable, through the gate at the back. Tom looked up at the bedroom window and breathed a sigh of relief. The curtains were tightly drawn. They were fast asleep inside. But Tom only felt safe when he was in the last of the fields behind the yard. He sprang into the saddle and gathered up the reins.

"Come on Chancey. We've only got an hour and there's a lot to do."

Chancey responded promptly to the light squeeze from Tom's calves and began to trot. Automatically, Tom turned him so they were heading for the beach. Gently, Chancey cantered along, and soon they were on the open stretches. Tom relaxed. This was fun.

At last they reached the clifftops. The tide was

out and the beach was deserted. The wind was whipping up the waves, billowing the water into clouds of spray. Tom leant back, putting his hand on Chancey's rump to steady himself as they picked their way down the path from the cliff.

Then they were down on the beach and suddenly they were galloping as though nothing else mattered... along the sand, through the waves and past the caves that he and Alex had discovered last summer. It was amazing. Tom found it hard to pull Chancey up when there was nothing to stop them from going on and on forever.

"Whoa boy, calm down," said Tom, clapping his hand to Chancey's neck and slowly pulling him up. Chancey snatched at the bit.

"That was to warm you up," Tom laughed. "We'll do some serious exercise now – serpentines. Ready?"

Chancey was jumpy as Tom tried to get him to make the 's' shape in the sand. But soon they had perfected the movement, bending from right to left, leaving a trail in the sand like a snake. Tom was miles away, when suddenly he realized how the time had flown.

"We must hurry back," he told Chancey, looking at his watch. "We'll ride in the outdoor school tomorrow… go through your paces and practise some jumping too."

Quietly, they rode back to Sandy Lane and stealthily crept into the yard. It was already twenty past seven. Luckily no one was around, but Tom promised himself to be more careful about timing in future. Quickly, he put Chancey in his stable.

"You're here early," boomed a voice behind him. Tom jumped. "Couldn't keep away from Chancey?" It was Nick.

"Um… I d-didn't sleep well, so I got up and thought I'd head down here," Tom stuttered.

Nick shook his head, smiling. He seemed unaware of anything out of the ordinary. Tom let out a sigh.

"Can you start doing the feeds?" Nick asked. "I've just put up the poster about the local show. It's only three weeks away. Good practice for Benbridge.

How about you riding Napoleon?"

Tom felt guilty. Napoleon had always been his favourite horse at the stables. Everyone said they were good together. But since Chancey had arrived... Tom couldn't feel the same about any other horse.

"Thanks Nick. I'll check it out," said Tom. He didn't dare ask if he could ride Chancey at the local show – he couldn't bear to hear Nick's refusal.

Nick looked puzzled. Normally Tom would have been rushing to sign up Napoleon. "I'm sorry, Tom. I haven't time to be with you and Chancey today. It'll have to be tomorrow," he said.

"Don't worry," said Tom. He turned away quickly, hoping Nick hadn't noticed him reddening. Tom hated going behind Nick's back. He hoped he could live with his conscience over the next few weeks.

Chapter 7

A Narrow Escape

As the date of the local show drew nearer, Tom was proved right about Nick: he never had enough time to take lessons, school Storm Cloud *and* help out with Chancey. So Tom continued his secret outings, not just to the beach, but in the outdoor school as well. It was risky there, as anyone coming early to Sandy Lane was bound to see them, but Chancey had to get used to an enclosed area. It was worth taking the risk, Tom thought.

That morning, Tom avoided leading Chancey down the drive to the outdoor school. It was the quickest way, but they could easily be heard at the cottage. Tom felt guilty as he rode the long way around through the fields. His heart beat faster. When they reached the outdoor school he calmed down and they quickly started to limber up, but after fifteen minutes of basic exercise, Chancey was obviously bored.

"OK. You've had enough," Tom said. "We'll try jumping." He dismounted, tethering Chancey to the railings while he organised the jumps.

Chancey snorted. Tom had raised the post and rails by two feet. "You want it higher? OK." Tom grinned, moving onto the next fence.

It took a while to raise all the jumps, and he knew he'd have to knock them down again once they'd finished. It was a nuisance, but he didn't want to get caught. Nick's last class the day before had been beginners and it would look highly suspicious if Tom left the jumps this high.

Chancey danced on the spot as Tom showed him the course. Tom nudged him on with his heels and carefully they eased their way around the course, clearing each jump in easy succession.

"Once more, Chancey," Tom whispered, turning the horse back to the start without stopping for a break.

Flying over the post and rails, Chancey then soared over the parallel bars. Landing lightly, Tom spun him on the spot for the treble on the far side of the school. Chancey didn't hesitate. He jumped fluently, his tail swishing as he touched down after the first and went on to clear the next two jumps.

Tom was always amazed at how high Chancey could go. Sometimes he thought he was asking too much, but Chancey never refused.

All too soon, Tom knew he ought to check his watch. "Time to stop," he groaned. "Or we might have company."

Dismounting, Tom led Chancey to his stable and untacked him. Then he raced back to the school to knock down the fences. Hurtling around the course, he kicked down the poles as he went, and strode into the yard.

"Morning Tom," Nick called from Hector's stable.

"Morning Nick," Tom replied breezily, as he strolled over to Chancey's stable. He wondered how long Nick had been there. A moment longer and they'd have been caught out.

"I've some free time after half nine. We could work with Chancey, if you like," said Nick.

"Brilliant," said Tom, trying to summon up enthusiasm. He wished he hadn't pushed Chancey so hard and hoped he wouldn't be too tired.

"Hi Tom," Jess called cheerfully from across the yard. "Could you help me with the feeds?"

"OK," Tom agreed. Together they set to work and by quarter to ten they had mucked out five stables, filled eight haynets and groomed the horses that were going to be used that morning. They reckoned they had done more than their fair share of work.

"Do you want to get Chancey ready?" Nick called.

"Sure," Tom answered, hurrying off.

Chancey looked puzzled when Tom started to tack him up again.

"Don't give us away, Chancey," Tom whispered in his horse's ear as he led him down to the school. Chancey snickered softly.

"Let's see what you can do, Tom," said Nick, opening the gate to the outdoor school. "Strange," he called. "I swear the jumps were all standing yesterday. Someone's been mucking around."

Tom felt embarrassed as Nick went around the course putting the jumps back up.

"Ready? Put him over the cross poles a couple of times to warm him up and then try this combination," said Nick. "You shouldn't find it difficult."

It was all the encouragement Tom needed. With a nudge of his heels, he urged Chancey on. Chancey cantered forward with long, easy strides, holding his head high, as he cleared the poles. Nick was mesmerised as he watched them moving gracefully around the paddock.

"I can't believe how well you're both going

together," Nick called. "It's a pleasure to watch. Each time that I've seen you both, there seems to be an overnight improvement. It's as if after each session Chancey thinks it all through and puts it into practice the next time. Look how he's perfected jumping that double."

So Nick had noticed a difference. Tom blushed. There was no overnight improvement. They'd been secretly practising the double for almost a week. What would Nick say if he found out?

Tom was nervous. His mother had been noticing things too. She'd complained Tom was spending too much time at Sandy Lane. She could easily say something to Nick and Sarah, worried Tom. He couldn't tell his mother Nick and Sarah didn't know he was there so early every morning. There was no alternative, he decided. He'd have to limit his sessions with Chancey.

As Tom led Chancey back to the yard, he thought how complicated it was. He didn't know how much longer he could go on. Training Chancey in secret was exhausting him. Nevertheless, Chancey was improving. Tom told himself that it would all be worth it in the end. Little did he know how close that end would be... that his plans were soon to be brought to an abrupt halt.

Chapter 8

The Warning

Over a week had passed and Chancey was playing up. When Tom asked him to canter, he trotted faster. When Tom told him to halt, he carried on walking. It was as though he was telling Tom he was bored. He'd never make a dressage horse, Tom realized. Better to give up the schooling and focus on jumping. Chancey was jumping beautifully.

Tom raised the treble. Was it asking too much?

It was a difficult combination, with only one horse stride between each of the jumps, but Chancey didn't hesitate as he approached the first. Sitting back on his hocks, he released himself through the air like a coil. Springing over the jumps, he cleared them one by one with at least a foot to spare. Tom couldn't remember ever feeling so exhilarated.

"Wait till Nick next trains us," he whispered. "He'll be amazed." And then Tom sighed. When would Nick train them again? Not that day. Nick had already told Tom he was too busy taking lessons.

Tom knew that he shouldn't grumble. Business was booming; exactly what Nick and Sarah needed. Tom was lost in thought when he sensed someone was watching. His heart skipped a beat.

It was Nick.

"Hello Tom," said Nick.

There was a strained silence.

"How long has this been going on?" There was no inflexion in Nick's voice for Tom to decide how to play things.

That was Nick all over, no words of reproach, just a composed question. Tom found Nick's restraint unnerving and tried to summon up courage.

"Nearly three weeks now. I didn't want to go behind your back, Nick. I had to." Tom swallowed hard. "We weren't going to be ready for Benbridge otherwise. Wait until you see Chancey. You won't be angry then," he said nervously.

"There will be no seeing him," replied Nick in a quiet rage. "What do you think you're playing at? I can't have you setting this example to the others. You could have been hurt. I'm responsible for you." Tom had never seen Nick so angry.

"I was trying to help. I didn't mean any harm," Tears welled in Tom's eyes. He rubbed them away, annoyed that he hadn't been able to stop himself. "Please look at him, Nick. He's brilliant. I only wanted to get him started. You've been so busy..."

There was an uncomfortable pause. Nick knew it was true. He'd been too tied up with other things to help Tom and Chancey, though he'd said he would. He felt a little guilty, but Tom had broken his promise. Nick thought long and hard. Should he let them show him what they could do?

"I shouldn't, Tom. But I'll give you one last chance," he said quickly, softening a little. "Eleven o'clock this morning, after the little ones' class. We'll take it from there." He turned away.

Tom trudged off to Chancey's stable, clutching a faint glimmer of hope.

"We'll show them." Tom gritted his teeth. He untacked Chancey and put out some food. When Chancey had finished eating, Tom began to groom him, starting with the legs and working up.

News spread quickly at Sandy Lane. Soon the others knew what had happened. They all felt sorry for Tom, but equally they couldn't believe what he'd done. None of them would have dared.

"Poor Tom," said Rosie.

"I thought something was going on," said Alex. "He's been really strange... so secretive."

The others nodded in agreement.

"We usually hang out together," Alex went on in a hurt voice. "And we haven't lately."

"I wonder how Chancey will be," said Jess. "Tom

must be confident if he's prepared to show Nick."

Tom did feel confident. That morning, Chancey had jumped the treble with ease. Nick *must* be too impressed to be angry. Then Tom could enter the local show on Chancey; they'd be able to use Chancey for lessons; everything would work out.

At ten to eleven, he went to get Chancey ready, Then he led him out of his stable and sprang confidently into the saddle.

"We'll try him in the school," Nick said.

As they headed down the drive, Chancey pirouetted, snorting as Tom gathered up the reins.

Nick opened the gate to the outdoor school. Suddenly Tom felt uneasy. Nick frowned. There was a sense of foreboding in the air and Tom felt his confidence ebbing away.

Tom never had a chance to show Nick what they could do. As the engine of a car roared in the distance, Chancey's ears flashed back and he started bucking like a maniac. Before he knew it, Tom was flung to the ground and Chancey was tearing towards the gate. He looked as though he was going to cannon straight into it. But without hesitating, he launched himself over it and charged down the road.

"Did you see that?" Alex cried excitedly. "Never mind him being crazy. That was a five-barred gate he cleared, with miles to spare."

Tom had landed heavily but the sand in the outdoor school had acted as a cushion. He sat still. His head was in his hands, his face was ashen, white with shock. Panic rose in his throat.

"What if he falls? He'll break his knees and then he'll be ruined. He'll have to be put down, and it will be all my fault. We have to catch him," he said, struggling to his feet.

"I knew something like this would happen," Nick said angrily. "He'll be far away by now. This was why I didn't want you riding him."

"He's been going so well for me," said Tom. "Maybe the sudden traffic noise startled him."

"Maybe he wasn't ready to be handled by a novice."

Nick's words stung Tom into realizing the enormity of what had happened.

"Let's go," said Nick. "We'll take the Land Rover. We have to find him. If he's on the road, if he causes an accident, Sandy Lane could lose its licence. Grab a head collar, Tom. I'll tell Sarah," he added, racing to the cottage.

Moments later they were rattling in the Land Rover down the drive and out of the yard.

"Keep looking, Tom," said Nick. "I'll drive slowly past the trees."

Tom couldn't see any movement in the thicket of pines. Chancey was nowhere to be seen. Nick drove on and on, but although there were plenty of horses in the surrounding fields, Chancey was not among them. Tom's heart missed a beat as he saw a chestnut horse, but his hopes sank as the horse's white face turned to look at him.

Two hours of solid driving, down every road and through every field that Nick could think of, and still they hadn't found him. Tom was in despair.

"Where can he be? We've tried everywhere," he wailed, his voice rising into hysteria.

"Calm down, Tom. He'll have to stop somewhere. We may as well go back to the stables. If there was any news, someone would have rung us by now," Nick said despondently.

As they turned into Sandy Lane, Rosie ran to meet them.

"Chancey's here! He's safe. Alex managed to catch him. He was grazing in the fields behind the stables. He must have found his own way home."

Tom raced to Chancey's stable to see for himself. Sure enough, there was Chancey, peacefully munching from a haynet as if nothing had happened. He looked up as Tom approached and whinnied softly. His eyes were bright and clear as his head cradled forward, nuzzling Tom for a titbit.

"No, Chancey. You're not having a reward today," Tom said furiously. The others crowded anxiously around Tom.

"Tom, he was amazing," said Alex, his eyes

glinting with excitement. "I can't believe how he cleared that gate. You were right. He really was born to jump."

A hush fell over the group as Nick approached. No one dared breathe as they waited to hear what he had to say.

"Well Tom," said Nick. "I forbade you to ride him before and I am forbidding you again. He's dangerous. If you disobey this time, then you'll not only be forbidden to ride Chancey, you'll be out of Sandy Lane... for good."

Chapter 9

The Local Show

It was so unfair, Tom thought. Really bad luck. Chancey had been doing so well for him in secret. It was the sudden car noise that had startled him. If Tom wasn't even allowed to ride Chancey, how could he ever prove that Chancey wasn't crazy? In the end, it was Alex who came up with the solution.

They were in the tack room, at dusk, cleaning tack. Nick was with a class and the others had all gone home.

"I'm sorry, Alex," said Tom. "I should have told

you what I was doing, but I didn't want you to feel you had to tell lies for me."

"I could have helped you," said Alex in a hurt voice. "I would have covered for you until you were absolutely ready to show Chancey to Nick."

"I thought we were," Tom said gloomily. "He'd been fantastic, until then. I don't know what to do."

"You've got to prove to Nick that all your training was worthwhile, that he is a great horse."

"How?"

Alex took a deep breath. "Well... ride him at the local show."

"No!" Tom spluttered. "You heard what Nick said. I'd be out of Sandy Lane."

"But if you know you're right about Chancey... You're riding Napoleon, aren't you?"

Tom nodded.

"Why not swap mounts? Ride Chancey instead? By the time Nick realizes what's happened, it'll be too late to stop you. And when you've won, you'll have proved your point. He can't be angry."

"He might be," said Tom. "And what happens if Chancey and I lose?"

"It's a risk you have to take. I'll help you," Alex continued. "I'm not riding in the open jumping so I can switch Napoleon's name for Chancey's at the show secretary's tent."

At first Tom was hesitant. But he was sure Alex was right, and as the days passed, he grew certain.

The yard buzzed with excitement on the day of the local show. The horses were washed, groomed and plaited. Tom groomed Chancey in secret and doubled back to collect him once everyone had left Sandy Lane. The show was only two miles away, so it didn't take Tom long to hack him over there.

Only ten minutes until Tom was due in the ring. Nervously, he paced up and down. No doubt the others would be looking for him, panicking as Napoleon stood unattended and riderless.

All he could do was wait, feeling sick as he thought of his ordeal. He'd gone over the course again and again in his mind. Chancey should be able to walk it. But they hadn't practised since Nick's warning.

Tom's hands felt clammy as he mounted and started to loosen Chancey up in the woods away from the showground. He mustn't let Chancey sense he was nervous. He had to stay calm. Tom buttoned his jacket and secured his chin strap.

"Number sixty-five... Tom Buchanan on Horton Chancellor," the voice called over the tannoy.

On the other side of the ring, Nick looked astonished.

Tom cantered over and acknowledged the judges. He rode a circle, waiting for the bell.

R-r-ring. Tom was off. His mind was focused on one goal – to jump clear. Nothing else was important. Nobody else mattered. Chancey looked magnificent as he headed for the first jump in a collected canter. His nostrils flared and his eyes flashed amber as he gathered his pace.

They were over the first and on to the gate. Tom felt Chancey speed up and tried to steady him.

Soaring over the gate, they approached the stile. They were clear. Turning back on themselves, they raced up the middle to jump the treble.

"One, two, three," Alex muttered as Chancey bounded over the fences. One more turn, then the parallel bars and finally the huge wall. Chancey leapt over the parallel bars nimbly and went on to fly over the wall, clearing it with ease. And then they were cantering through the finish to the sound of applause, as the voice announced the result.

"Tom Buchanan on Horton Chancellor, jumping clear with no time faults and into the jump-off."

They were through to the next round.

"Well done, boy. You were brilliant," Tom grinned, patting Chancey's neck as the spectators looked on admiringly. Then he saw Nick.

Nick's eyes flashed angrily. "Finish the jump-off and see me afterwards, Tom."

Tom looked at him pleadingly, feeling sick again. They must win.

Four competitors remained in the jump-off, and

Tom was third in the ring. He watched the other competitors, weighing up the opposition. The first one had a bad round sending everything hurtling to the floor. The second, a girl in immaculate cream jodhpurs and navy hacking jacket, looked incredibly professional and for a moment Tom's confidence crashed. She jumped clear.

Then it was Tom's turn. He cantered the obligatory circle, looked determinedly straight ahead and approached the first.

There was a loud bang as Chancey rapped the top rail. Tom's heart sank. He looked under his arm and saw the pole was still hanging there – how, he didn't know. The near miss startled Chancey and he went on to clear the gate by miles, careful to pick his feet up as they flew over it. Collecting his stride, Tom faced Chancey at the stile, leaning forward to take his weight off his back. Tucking his legs up under him, Chancey sailed over the jump.

Tom swung him round neatly to race up the middle for the treble. Chancey cleared the three jumps with ease. Tom knew how far he could push him and with another sharp turn, Chancey sprang gracefully over the parallel bars. Now there was only the wall. The crowd held their breath as horse and rider soared. They were over it!

Everyone cheered as the voice announced that Tom Buchanan and Horton Chancellor had taken the lead with a time of three minutes and sixteen seconds.

"No one will beat that," Alex said excitedly to a stranger standing next to him. He was correct; the last rider couldn't beat Tom's time. Moments later Tom was galloping around the ring, a red rosette attached to Chancey's bridle.

Nick was the first to meet him coming out of the ring. Tom looked shame-faced.

"Well done, Tom. You were both magnificent," he grinned. Watching Tom had reminded Nick of how he'd been as a boy. When he realized that he would have done exactly the same, his anger melted away.

"You've proved your point," he continued. "You'll

be representing Sandy Lane at Benbridge."

Tom felt something between triumph and exhaustion. All his worries about Nick's reaction and his early morning stints had finally caught up with him.

"Everybody wanted to know who Chancey was," said Kate. "You'll probably get good offers for him after that amazing performance."

Kate's words rang alarm bells in Tom's head. Of course people would be interested in Chancey – he was an exceptional horse. But Chancey belonged to Georgina. Tom sighed. His win didn't mean total triumph after all. It had echoes of loss. For Benbridge was the beginning of the end. The end of summer, and the end of his time with Chancey.

Chapter 10

An Unwanted Visitor

Tom knew the competition at Benbridge would be much tougher than the local show. Chancey would have to be at his very best to have any hope of winning. He also knew he had to speak to Nick.

"I was wondering if you'd like to use Chancey in lessons now," he began hesitantly.

"That's generous, Tom," Nick said thoughtfully.

Tom's face dropped. Chancey had to pay his way at Sandy Lane, but Tom hated the thought of anyone else riding him.

"But now he's grown used to you, only you should

ride him," Nick went on, "certainly until Benbridge. Besides, we don't need him. Feather's back in action and Storm Cloud is doing well."

Tom breathed a sigh of relief and strolled over to the hay bales to join Alex and Jess. He took out the packed lunch his mother now made him to take to Sandy Lane, like the other helpers. She had finally agreed it was unreasonable for Tom to race back home to eat, only to tear out again to the stables.

They munched happily, as they spread out the Benbridge entry form.

"Which classes are you entering, Tom?" asked Kate, as she and Rosie strolled over.

"Only the open jumping. Chancey can't stand still enough for the show classes," Tom laughed.

"I've entered everything," said Kate. "I want Jester plastered with rosettes – though we've probably got the best chance in the showing."

"I hope at least you win the potato race," said Rosie, giggling.

They were all together now, the Sandy Lane

regulars. Nick had selected Tom, Kate and Alex to ride at Benbridge, but Rosie and Jess intended to go as well to support their friends.

Tom looked at his watch. Half two. He had to work with Chancey. Sarah was taking the others down to the beach for a ride. Tom loved the beach, but Nick had offered to train them for an hour in the school. And with Benbridge less than two weeks away, it was an offer he couldn't refuse.

Chancey's head appeared over the door as Tom held out the carrot that his mother had packed. He smiled. Perhaps she was starting to feel some affection for his four-legged friend. Chancey stretched out his neck and sniffed appreciatively, his silky lips mumbling delicately over Tom's flat hand. It made Tom laugh to see Chancey so careful with his food yet so bold when he jumped. Tom tacked him up and led him out into the yard.

"See you later, Tom," Sarah called. "Tell Nick we'll be back by four. No later, anyway, as high tide is at four."

"OK," Tom answered. "I'll tell him."

At low tide, the wide expanse of beach at Sandy Bay was clear, but when the tide came in, the sand flooded. If you weren't careful, you could find yourself cut off. Nick always posted a monthly copy of tide times on the tack room door and made everyone check it before a ride to the beach.

"Let's go, Tom," said Nick, stepping out of the tack room. "See what you make of the course I've set up for you in the outdoor school. There's one difficult jump. But I think you should manage it."

Nick had erected a figure of eight jumps for them to practise over in the outdoor school. The white railings looked crisp in the bright sunshine, contrasting sharply with the gaily painted fences. Chancey eyed the course suspiciously. The difficult jump proved to be a square oxer.

"Parallel bars – hard for a horse to judge the stretch and clear," Tom muttered.

"I'll watch you for a while, Tom," said Nick, jumping up onto the railings, "but then I have to take a private hack."

Tom trotted Chancey around the school in an easy canter.

"Go round once more, Tom," said Nick. "It'll make him more balanced when he starts jumping and settle his rhythm."

"OK," said Tom and swiftly they cantered around the circuit.

"Ready now?" Nick called. "Approach the first two jumps at a trot. It's good training for him."

Tom popped Chancey over the post and rails. Trotting him over the stile, he turned him wide at the corner of the school to give him enough time to see the square oxer. Chancey had been concentrating and, with encouragement from Tom, stepped up his pace to leap over the jump, clearing it easily. Relieved, Tom rode across the school on a diagonal for the double.

"Try not to anticipate the jump and lean forward too early, Tom," Nick suggested. "Let Chancey find his natural take-off point, otherwise you'll unbalance him and he'll try to put in an extra stride. Then you'll be the one who's unbalanced," he added, laughing. "Otherwise, it's good. It's as if he's a different horse."

"He's always like this with me now, Nick," Tom replied. "He trusts me."

"I think you're right. Try him again," said Nick. "Then I really have to go and take this lesson."

Tom and Chancey soared around the course, unaware that Nick had left. Jump after jump was cleared in swift succession until eventually Tom pulled Chancey to a halt. Leaping to the ground, he tethered him to the railings.

"That was just for practice," he said mischievously, as he went round the course raising the jumps. "This will be better."

Tom lost all sense of time when he jumped Chancey. Now, he was so involved with his riding, that he didn't notice the girl watching them in the shadows. Sulkily, she stared at them as she took in the scene.

The only sound was Chancey's hooves pounding

against the ground as horse and rider sailed over the jumps. Happy with their success, Tom jumped off Chancey to raise the jumps again, not satisfied until he had stretched them both to the limit.

"That's it for now, boy," he said, as they knocked down a jump in the last round. "You're exhausted." Chancey's sides were puffing in and out like bellows. "I don't want to push you too far."

He slid off the horse as the girl stepped out from the shadows. Tom was startled. The sun shone in his eyes as he returned her stony gaze.

"Georgina?" he gasped. "What on earth are you doing here?"

Chapter 11

From Bad to Worse

Georgina was standing right in front of him. Her cold blue eyes froze him. What was she doing here? She wasn't due back for another three weeks. "I've come back early so I can ride Horton Chancellor at the Benbridge show," Georgina announced.

Tom stared at his cousin's defiant face, his heart thumping. His worst nightmare was coming true.

"A-Are you taking him home with you today?" he stammered.

"Oh no," Georgina said haughtily. "Change of plan. Daddy's tired of having him at home. I have to arrange with the owners of Sandy Lane to keep him here at half-livery. Do you know them?"

Tom nodded, as his mind raced. Benbridge... keeping him at Sandy Lane... half-livery... "I'll take you to meet Nick," he mumbled, still in shock. "Do you want to take Chancey to his stable?"

"No, you can do it," said Georgina breezily. "I'll have plenty of time with him later."

"OK. Oh, here's Nick now," he said as Nick strode towards them.

"What's going on?" Nick asked.

"This is my cousin, Georgina," said Tom, holding on to a rather jumpy Chancey. "She owns Horton Chancellor. She would like to talk to you about the possibility of keeping him at livery with you."

"I see," said Nick thoughtfully. "Hi, Georgina. You'd better come and discuss things at the cottage with my wife Sarah." He tried to catch Tom's eye, but Tom had already turned away.

"So that's it, boy," said Tom, alone with Chancey. "Your owner has come back to claim you."

Tom felt numb. He'd never really thought beyond this summer, though he had known it loomed ahead. If he was honest, he had half-hoped Georgina would never come back, that she would forget about Chancey altogether. Unrealistic dreams. He sighed.

"What's the matter, Tom?" asked Rosie, leaning over the stable door.

"It's my cousin, Georgina," Tom said sadly. "She's back from her holiday."

"That's early, isn't it?" The words tumbled from Rosie's mouth before she could stop them.

"Yes it is," said Tom, turning away. Rosie saw the hurt in his eyes and wished she knew what to say to make him feel better. She hung around for a short time, then scuttled away, still unable to find the right words.

Tom didn't have to wait long. Nick wanted to find Tom before he decided anything. He understood the bond between Tom and Chancey.

"Are you OK, Tom? I suppose you knew she was

coming back sometime. It's been a shock, though, hasn't it? I could say that there's no room to stable him here if that makes it easier for you?"

"No, thanks," said Tom quickly. "At least if he's here I can still see him."

"They want him kept at half-livery," said Nick. "So you can ride him when Georgina isn't here. I've bad news, though. She's insisting that she rides him at Benbridge."

"I know," Tom said bitterly.

"I told her about the work you'd done – the rights and wrongs of it all – but she wasn't interested," said Nick. "Listen Tom, if it's any consolation, I'm entered on Feather for the open jumping at Benbridge. I'd like you to ride her instead."

"But..."

"No buts," said Nick. "You'd be representing Sandy Lane." Tom nodded in hesitant acceptance as he turned for home.

Tom's mother knew immediately that something was wrong when he trudged into the kitchen.

"Tom? Are you all right? What's happened? You look as if you've seen a ghost."

"Almost true," said Tom. "Georgina's back."

"But she's not due back for another three weeks."

"Sh-she came back to ride at the Benbridge show," he stammered.

Mrs. Buchanan couldn't bear the look of disappointment on Tom's face. He'd talked about nothing but Benbridge for weeks. But she knew Georgina. When Georgina wanted something, she went all out to get it.

"Perhaps Nick would let you ride one of the other horses," she suggested, knowing this offered no real consolation.

"He already has," said Tom. "But it's not the same."

Tom woke the next morning with a heavy heart. The blue sky promised a scorching summer's day. He had to put on a brave face and go down to Sandy Lane. Benbridge was only ten days away. He owed it to Feather. On the count of ten, he sighed and forced himself out of bed.

When Tom arrived, it was 10 o'clock and Chancey was still waiting to be groomed.

"What's going on Nick?" asked Tom furiously.

"I'm equally curious. Georgina gave strict instructions to leave him alone. She said that she'd be down here to look after him. She's probably overslept."

"I'll do it," said Tom.

He was getting the last pieces of straw out of Chancey's tail when Georgina sauntered into the stable yard.

"You're late," snapped Tom. "If you've got a horse, you have responsibilities."

"I don't have to answer to you," Georgina crowed. "You're not my mother." Her blue eyes flashed scornfully at him. "Nick, I'm booked in for the beach ride this morning, aren't I?" She grabbed the brush from Tom as Nick passed by.

"That's right," he replied.

Tom groaned. He was due to ride Feather for the beach ride. Kate was on Jester, Jess on Minstrel,

Rosie was riding Pepper and Alex was on Hector –
all on their favourite horses. Tom didn't intend to
give it up because of Georgina being there. Besides,
he needed to spend time with Feather, for Benbridge.

"OK," said Nick, as everyone gathered round.
"For those who are new to Sandy Lane... Georgina,
can you please listen?"

"OK," she said sulkily, pulling her hair into a pony
tail as her reins trailed by Chancey's side.

Nick started again. "For all of you who don't know,
there are strict rules about riding on the beach.
First, always keep behind the horse in front of you.
Secondly, although it's not applicable this morning,
always check the tide sheet on the tack room door
when planning a ride to the beach. The tide rolls in
very fast on this stretch of the coast and you could
find yourselves cut off. At the very latest, you must
be at the path to the cliffs by the time the water
reaches Gull Rock, which is half an hour before high
tide. Sandy Lane will not accept responsibility for
anyone disobeying these rules. Is that clear?"

"Yes Nick," came back a chorus of voices.

"Then let's go." Turning Whispering Silver, Nick led the riders out of the yard in single file. Tom shuddered as he saw Georgina jab Chancey in the mouth. Now she was pulling on the reins *and* driving him on with her heels. No wonder Chancey was confused. Tom had to look away.

The August sun warmed their backs. Tom looked behind him at the line of trotting horses as they crossed the coastal track to the open stretches. It was a lovely sight. Tom could smell the salt in the air as they cantered along the cliff tops.

Tom gazed down at the beach below as Feather sniffed the air. Slowly, the horses picked their way down the cliff path. Once on the sand, Chancey seemed even more edgy. Georgina yanked at his head as they trotted along the shoreline.

"Try not to fight with him for his head, Georgina," Nick called out. Georgina scowled and sawed furiously on the reins. Chancey's neck tightened. He was beginning to foam at the mouth and the hollows of his nostrils were a blood red as he struggled against his leash. Tom looked on grimly.

"Right, let's canter," said Nick. "Remember, it's not a race. Alex, you start, and we'll follow on."

Alex pushed Hector on into a stiff canter, setting a pace for the others to follow. Soon they were streaming along behind him. Minstrel followed on Hector's toes, then came Kate, Rosie, Georgina and Tom. Nick brought up the rear with Whispering Silver.

And then Tom saw Georgina push Chancey on into a gallop. They had overtaken a startled Rosie and were wildly out of control as they overtook Kate and Jess and went neck and neck with Hector. Thinking it was a race, the horses bolted along the beach in a stampede. Tom tried to pull Feather back gently but he couldn't stop her. His face felt taut as the wind whistled past.

Eventually, Chancey seemed to be tiring. He slowed down, cantering... trotting... walking.... Tom breathed a sigh of relief. Nick was going to be furious but at least they'd stopped. The others drew to a halt behind him. Rosie looked as white as a sheet.

"Georgina, did you listen to a word I said?" Nick asked angrily.

"Yes," she replied insolently. "But I didn't want to go so slowly all through the ride."

"As long as you ride at Sandy Lane, you ride under my rules," Nick roared. "Is that clear?"

"OK," said Georgina, smirking as he turned away.

Nick led the riders back to Sandy Lane, silent but obviously angry. Tom felt as though a black cloud hung over him. He hated seeing Chancey pushed on like that. He couldn't bear to see the horse ruined. He decided to keep out of Chancey and Georgina's way. He'd still visit Chancey with a daily titbit, but he'd make sure he wasn't in classes with them.

Nine days now to the Benbridge show. He would spend more time with Feather. She didn't have Chancey's strength and courage, but she was a talented horse. Tom was sure that they would do well at Benbridge.

Chapter 12

Benbridge!

The yard was busy on the morning of the Benbridge show. Everyone was rushing around oiling hooves, searching for grooming kit, plaiting manes, putting studs in hooves. By nine o'clock, everyone was ready with the last of the horses boxed and bolted.

In spite of everything, Tom felt excited. Feather was easily the best of Nick and Sarah's horses. And at least Chancey was going to Benbridge, even if they wouldn't be sharing the same experience. He was glad he didn't have to share the journey with

Georgina. Nick had tactfully thought that Tom and Georgina in the horse box together was too much, so suggested Sarah took her with the others in the Land Rover. Georgina had complained that she hadn't expected Chancey to share a horse box. Nick had soon silenced her by telling her that neither of them had to be taken to the show.

Of the Sandy Lane team, Kate had entered Jester for the 13.2 show class, Alex had entered Hector for the novice jumping and Tom and Georgina were down for the open jumping. Tom hoped people wouldn't think Georgina was Sandy Lane trained because she was arriving with them. Her aggressive riding style wouldn't help the stables' reputation.

As they arrived, Tom's eyes widened. He'd forgotten what a big show was like. It was so official, so serious. Entries were being announced over a loudspeaker. Officials were running around. There was a stand for the judges. It even *smelled* important. Tom felt a knot in his stomach.

A steward glanced at their car park label and

waved them on their way. Nick halted the horse box under the shade of a tree and Tom sprang from the cab, quickly putting down the ramp to let out the horses. He was leading Chancey out when the Land Rover pulled up next to them and Georgina opened the door and jumped out.

"Give him here," she cried, grabbing the head collar from Tom. Chancey's eyes rolled as she yanked his head to the ring on the side of the horse box.

"Be careful with him, Georgina," advised Alex. "You know how jumpy he can get."

"Who says you're boss?" sneered Georgina. "A horse has to know who's in control."

"Don't let's spoil such a wonderful day by squabbling," soothed Kate. "Come on everyone, we have to collect our entry numbers. Tom, you and Georgina should let them know of your change of horses."

"You're right," said Tom. They picked up their numbers from the secretary's tent, and fastened them on carefully.

"They're vast," said Kate laughing. "It'll cover my whole back."

"That's the general idea," said Georgina.

"I wish she'd shut up," Kate muttered under her breath. "She's such a know-all."

Tom said nothing. He was used to Georgina. He wasn't going to let her get to him... not today.

"Can someone help me with my hair?" Kate asked. "I can't get it all in this hair net. I wish we didn't have to wear them."

Tom laughed, as Rosie went to the rescue. "I won't see you before the showing, Kate," he said. "It's on the other side of the ground to the jumping, so good luck."

"You too," she smiled.

Tom hurried to inspect the course. The jumps weren't huge, but it was a stiff course with difficult combinations – eleven jumps in all. Adrenaline began to surge through his body as he thought of what lay ahead.

Back at the horse box, he found his parents had

arrived with Georgina's, and were having lunch with the Sandy Lane group. Tom was amazed at Georgina's capacity to eat. He felt sick with dread.

"Hi Tom," said his Uncle Bob. "Thanks for looking after the horse while we've been away. Apparently you've done a fantastic job with the brute."

Tom frowned at the word "brute." Tom's mother glanced at him sympathetically.

"You're looking good, Tom," she said, quickly changing the subject.

"Thanks Mum," he said looking down at his newly-pressed jodhpurs. He winced as he stretched his shoulders. Until that moment he'd forgotten that his hacking jacket was too small for him and extremely uncomfortable. He'd rather be wearing his old mucking-out clothes any day.

"Georgina, have you walked the course yet?" he asked.

"No, don't need to," said Georgina, her mouth crammed full of cheese sandwich. "I've seen it. Looks fine."

"OK," said Tom, with a shrug. "Well, I'm off to loosen up Feather. I'll be at the collecting ring if anyone wants me. The jumping's started."

"Good luck, Tom," Mrs. Buchanan called, as Tom walked over to Chancey.

"Good luck, boy," he whispered to Chancey, pulling his ears gently. Chancey nudged him playfully, shifting his weight lazily from one foot to the other as he basked in the sun.

Tom went to Feather and carefully tacked her up. One of her plaits had come loose, so Tom rapidly restitched it. Time was moving on and his nerves were even worse. He was sure that the horse would be able to feel the tension running through his body.

Quickly, he mounted and walked Feather to the collecting ring where a terrifying amount of professional-looking riders were limbering up their mounts. Over a hundred competitors had entered the open jumping class. It was the most popular event of the day. As Tom started to warm Feather up, Alex came riding past on Jester.

"Sixth," he called, grinning. Tom was pleased for him. Sixth was good at a show of this standard.

"There's hope for me, maybe," he yelled back as Alex trotted on towards the gymkhana events.

Then came the announcement over the speaker that brought Tom back to reality.

"Name change... number sixty-two, Horton Chancellor, owned by Robert Thompson, will be ridden by Georgina Thompson and number sixty-eight, Feather, owned by Sandy Lane Stables, will be ridden by Tom Buchanan," rang out over the speaker.

Tom gritted his teeth and listened to the numbers being announced. They were up to fifty-eight already. Chancey's turn soon, and Georgina wasn't here. Usually Tom didn't like to watch anyone else riding the course, but he had to watch Chancey.

Jumping off Feather, he led her to the horse box and tied her to a ring before going to the stands. The crowd was quiet as competitor number sixty picked his way carefully around the course, finishing well within the three minute time limit. Tom stood away from his parents. He didn't want to hear any sympathetic noises from them as Georgina jumped Chancey. He was also in two minds about his feelings. He wanted Chancey to do well and yet he half-wanted Georgina to do badly.

Here they were now. Tom watched intently as Horton Chancellor was called into the ring and cantered a circle. Then they were off. Tom shivered as he heard the loud crack of the whip strike against Chancey's rump. Chancey looked equally displeased and almost leapt out of his skin with fright. He threw himself over the first jump, clearing it by miles. Georgina only just managed to regain her composure in time to sit still for the shark's teeth and the bank. They were over them, but at a punishing pace.

"Steady boy, steady," Tom breathed.

But it was too late, they were charging towards the combination, and now Georgina was kicking him on. Suddenly, she tried to check Chancey as he was about to jump the parallel. Tom closed his eyes as he heard the loud rap echo around the ring, but somehow the pole stayed up. They were rushing on to the treble. Georgina shortened her reins. Tom couldn't bear to look as Chancey struggled for his head and lurched over the three fences... clear.

She turned him stiffly towards the next jump. She wasn't going to be so lucky this time. There wasn't a moment for Chancey to gather impetus and, with a loud bang, he hit the gate which was sent crashing to the floor. Another loud whack resounded from Georgina's whip as Chancey headed for the last two jumps. Chancey lunged forward for the stile and staggered over it, his hooves just clipping the top. Then he reeled onto the gate. He was over it. But by the time he was through the finish, Chancey was foaming at the mouth and looked a nervous wreck. His body was drenched in sweat. Tom turned away in disgust at the sight of her parents congratulating her as the speaker announced that competitor number sixty-two had four faults.

Tom tried to compose himself as he collected

Feather, blotting out what he had seen. He worked out that they probably had about half an hour until it was their turn. Tom mounted and turned into the collecting ring. He trotted Feather around and then, with a light nudge, took her into a gentle canter. She had a lovely loping stride, a very easy canter to ride. Gently, she glided over the post and rails that were set up as a practice jump.

"Not long now," he told her, patting her shoulder as he slowed her down. Calmly, Tom walked Feather around the ring to settle her as they awaited their turn. He could see another competitor come trotting out of the ring. And then suddenly it was upon them.

Once Tom was called into the ring, he told himself to focus. They were here to do their best, and that was all they could do.

The bell rang out and they cantered to the first. Tom eased Feather over the brush, and they approached the shark's teeth. Deftly, she sprang over it. And now it was the bank. Taking it all in her stride, she rode onto it and down the other side.

Tom swung her round wide to the combination, giving her enough room to look at it. He sat tight to the saddle, determined not to make the same mistakes Georgina had. Gently, he rode Feather to the middle of the jumps, steadying her as she sailed over them. He was so light with his hands, she could hardly have known he was there. Tom was starting to enjoy himself.

Leisurely, he faced her at the treble and they soared over the three jumps in succession. Again, he swooped around in a large circle to take Feather over the gate, the stile, the wall. Touch down! There was a loud cheer from the crowd as they left the ring. Tom clapped his hand to Feather's shoulder and buried his head in her mane.

"You were brilliant," he mumbled.

The speaker announced the result.

"Tom Buchanan on Feather, jumping clear with no time faults."

"Well done," called Rosie, who was jumping up and down with excitement.

Tom was going to have to wait until the jump-off, so he wandered over to where his parents were watching the rest of the competitors.

"Well done, Tom," his mother cried. She couldn't believe how well he had ridden.

"You took your time, Tom," Georgina sneered spitefully. "It must be easy to jump clear if you go at that snail's pace. You'll have to be a bit faster next time if you don't want to be laughed out of the ring." Tom had to bite his tongue to stop himself from being very rude. Still Georgina went on.

"Horton Chancellor and I were rather unlucky to knock that gate, weren't we?" she said, not waiting for a reply. "He overran it rather. Still, less competition for you in the jump-off, eh?"

Tom was fuming, but he didn't have enough time to be angry, as the voice announced that there were ten riders through to the jump-off and the jumps were being raised that very moment. Tom rushed forward to watch.

The course was enormous now and speed was

going to be crucial. He was the fifth one in. Not as good a position as he'd had at the local show, but still better than being first. The competition seemed pretty stiff. The other riders all looked as though they had been competing for years. Tom could hardly bear to watch, never mind listen, as the riders went into the ring and the results were announced. All the times sounded very fast. Tom didn't have a clue what he needed to beat as he entered the ring for the second time. He would just do his best.

"Good luck Tom!" Rosie and Jess called from behind the rails.

Tom couldn't hear them though. The crowd hushed as he circled Feather.

And then they were off... racing to the first as the clock began ticking its countdown. They sailed over the brush, and then raced over the shark's teeth and soared over the bank. Feather's black eyes gleamed and her ears were pricked as she arched her neck. Her Arab lines were clearly defined as she stretched out her stride and raced forward. All Tom could see were the fences ahead of him, all he could hear was the sound of pounding hooves. Tom turned Feather to the combination. There were no wide swoops this time. The crowd gasped at the sharpness of the turn, but Feather knew what was expected of her and didn't even hesitate at the combination. Tom rode her at the middle of the jump, propelling her forward with his legs and she tucked her feet up under her as if the poles were hot pokers.

Again, Tom turned her immediately they touched the ground, so that there was hardly enough time for them to gather momentum. But he had judged it just right and Feather surged forward for the treble. One, two, three. Tom leaned forward in the saddle as the horse found her natural take-off and swiftly cleared the fences. Now there were only three more jumps. It was all happening so quickly. Feather cantered on the spot, preparing herself for the last turn. Tom steadied her as they approached the gate. Cleared. Then they were on to the stile. Cleared. Now they were approaching the huge wall. They were over, and at what a speed!

Adrenaline was still coursing through Tom as the voice from the speaker announced that he had taken the lead with a time of three minutes and four seconds. Tom clapped his hand to Feather's neck in excitement and jumped to the floor.

"You were awesome, Tom," called Jess, whose knuckles were white with tension. "I bet you've won it."

Tom shook his head. "Someone's sure to beat me. There are still four competitors to go."

"I'm not so sure," said Nick. "That will be a hard act to follow. Well done."

Tom walked Feather to the trees to cool down. He could hardly believe he had jumped clear. And he didn't want to watch the remaining competitors. It seemed unsportsmanlike to hope they wouldn't do well.

It seemed to take forever. The speaker repeatedly called out the times, each time announcing that Tom held the lead. Only two more riders to go. Tom held his breath at the gasps from the crowd as the competitors thundered around the course. But no one matched his time.

Tom was stunned when his name was called as the winner. Somehow, he found himself flying around the ring again, this time with a red rosette pinned to Feather's bridle and a huge silver cup in his hands. Beams of light sprang off it as it glinted in the sunlight and they galloped their lap of honour. This had to be the greatest moment of his life.

As he came out of the ring, all his friends from Sandy Lane gathered around him. He felt it was a dream... He, Tom Buchanan, winner of the open jumping at Benbridge. And then his heart sank as he remembered who he should have been riding.

"Chancey," he whispered. "I should have been riding Chancey."

Chapter 13

To the Rescue

"I can't believe Georgina's parents congratulated her on her performance at Benbridge. She rode like she was wearing spurs. Chancey would have won the open jumping if Tom had been riding him." Alex didn't sound mean; he never bad-mouthed anyone. He sounded as if he was just stating facts.

"Georgina is just a show-off," said Jess, wrinkling her nose.

"She's going to keep Chancey on at Sandy Lane too. It's hard for Tom." Alex brushed the last traces of sawdust from Hector's tail.

"At least he gets to see Chancey," said Jess. "Tom loves that horse. He's transformed him. Do you remember what he was like when he first arrived at Sandy Lane?"

Jess and Alex were still chatting away when Tom passed behind them. They didn't know he'd heard every word.

Tom couldn't stop thinking about Chancey at Benbridge. The horse had been driven into a total frenzy and he was in no position to say anything. He shouldn't have let himself get so attached. He hadn't meant to. It had just happened that way. He hadn't realized how hard it would be to give him up.

As Tom untacked Feather, he glanced around the yard. Everything was in order, everything was in its correct place. Except Chancey's stable door was wide open and swinging in the wind.

Bang! Ominously, it slammed shut.

Probably Georgina had forgotten to bolt it. Tom stuck his head round the door. The stable was empty – neither Chancey nor his tack were there. It didn't make sense. Georgina couldn't be riding in the woods. He'd just been there on his hack. She hated practising, so she wouldn't be in the outdoor school. Tom raced down the drive to check it out, just in case, but the outdoor school was deserted.

Then, as he turned back to the yard, he guessed. Georgina must have taken Chancey to the beach. Tom remembered her impatience with the last coastal ride. She would love an opportunity to ride Chancey far out on the beach with no one to stop her. He looked at his watch. A quarter past four. He had a horrible feeling that high tide was at five today. The beach would be almost covered by now.

He ran to the tack room and looked at the tide sheet, hoping that he was wrong. He felt the blood rushing to his head as he studied it. Yes. He'd been right, and he wished he hadn't been. Silly girl.

"Nick," he yelled, racing to the cottage for help. But no one was around. Alex and Jess has disappeared too. There wasn't a moment to lose. He grabbed a bridle and ran to Feather's stable. He'd have to go himself. Pulling the horse's head up out of her feed bowl, he put the bridle back on and led her out of the stable. No time for a saddle. He opened the gate and vaulted onto her back. Feather's neck was arched and her tail was held high as she whinnied excitedly.

Tom turned her and pushed her on... faster and faster until they were galloping. Now they were at the gate on the other side of the field. He couldn't waste time stopping to open it. Gritting his teeth as they went forward, he drove Feather towards the hedgerow. He grimaced as he heard the sharp twigs scratch her belly. He felt himself slipping and gripped harder with his knees. Feather took it as a command to go faster and started to gallop over the stubble at a furious pace. Tom clung on desperately as they tore through the woods, on and on to the open stretches beyond.

It was only when they were on the cliff tops that Tom drew Feather to a halt and looked down at the beach below. It was almost covered, except for a few remaining islands of sand left amidst the surging, swirling sea. A shimmering expanse of water stretched out in front of him.

Tom listened carefully. All he could feel was his heart beating faster, all he could hear was the ominous cry of the gulls. He squinted into the distance. Perhaps they weren't here after all.

And then he heard a pitiful cry coming from a sand bar some way beyond Gull Rock. Straining his eyes, he could just make out a person and a horse, the water seeping around them. The horse was sweating and frantically swishing his tail. Georgina and Chancey. It had to be.

"Georgina!" yelled Tom. Why didn't she guide Chancey to the shore? It was probably still within their depth. And horses were good swimmers. They could do it if they were quick. Tom felt helpless. What could he do? If he and Feather swam out to them, the tide would be even higher. They'd never get back. And he knew that he wasn't strong enough to swim it alone.

Out of desperation, the solution came to him. If he rode around towards the headland, he could climb down the blowhole into the caves that he and Alex had explored last summer, and then wade across the rocks to the sand bar. Without hesitating, he gathered up Feather's reins and pushed her forward. Deftly she raced along the cliff tops to the far side of the bay, picking her way through the loose stones as she went. Tom dismounted. There was nowhere to tie her. He knotted her reins, slapped her rump and sent her on her way, hoping she'd head back to Sandy Lane and raise the alarm.

Soon he found what he was looking for. Tom shuddered as he looked down into the black abyss below him.

"OK," he said to himself. He knew he could get down. He'd done it loads of times with Alex. But this was different – he had to be quick and accurate. One slip and he'd crash to the bottom of the hole.

Tom was clutching at the stumps of grass. His knuckles were white, and he was trembling. Down he climbed into the hole. He knew there were foot holds cut out of the rock. He tried to feel for them. Think of it as a ladder, he said to himself as he inched himself down and down.

Finally his feet touched water. He'd done it. Now he looked around him. Holding onto weed and rocks to steady himself, he waded out of the cave against the waves until he was up to his hips in the swirling current.

"Georgina," he screamed. And this time she heard him. Her face was contorted with fear.

"I'm coming for you," he said, steadily. The water was at his waist; a wave rolled in and he was up to his neck. But he was nearly there. He'd have to swim the last bit. Not far, he told himself. And then he reached the sand bar.

"Quick, Georgina. The tide's still coming in. The sand bar will be covered in a moment."

"What do I do?" she wailed, panic rising in her throat, her eyes white with fear. "Where did you come from?"

"Keep calm," said Tom. "I came from a cave over there at the side of the cliff," he pointed. "If we can get back, then there's a hole you can climb up."

"No, no," she wailed. "I'm not going in the water. I'll drown. You should have got them to send a boat for me."

"Who? Get real, Georgina," said Tom. "There wasn't time for a boat. No one knows you're here."

The sand bar had halved in size since he had first spotted them and they were running out of time. Fast.

"I'll swim to the cave and you hold onto my shoulders," Tom said, desperately trying to remember his life-saving classes.

Georgina's panic was subsiding. "OK, I'll hold onto you and you drag me."

"Right," said Tom, getting more impatient by the minute. "Let's go."

"Chancey," he called. "Chancey, I'm coming back for you. Don't do anything silly."

The horse was sidestepping around the sand bar,

his eyes rolling uncontrollably.

Tom strode into the waves and plunged forward as Georgina grabbed him. She was clinging on so tightly, that at first he panicked that she would drag him under. Once they'd started, she calmed down, and her grip slackened. Doggedly, Tom swam forward. It seemed like forever, until eventually they could stand.

"Walk forward, Georgina. Your feet can touch the bottom here." Quickly, he led her into the cave.

"This is the hole," he said pointing upwards. "Come on, up you go."

"I'm not going up there."

"Yes you are," Tom said firmly. "Or you'll drown."

"I need you to show me how to do it," Georgina cried hysterically.

"I've got to go back for Chancey, Georgina."

"Never mind the horse," she screamed. "What about *me*?" Tom looked at her in disbelief.

"I'll drown," she said. "He's only a horse, he can be replaced."

Tom looked out to sea at the familiar figure still struggling on the sand bar, now a silhouette against the bleak horizon. A lump blocked his throat.

He swallowed. "No," he told her. "I'm going back. I've got to get him. If I guide him, we can swim to the path. I've got you this far. Once you're on the top of the cliffs, you'll be safe. You know the way back."

"It's dangerous," Georgina yelled.

But Tom didn't listen. He headed back into the sea. In an instant he was up to his neck. He spluttered as he gulped a mouthful of water. He wished he'd stripped off his sweatshirt, as the weight of water-logged material made moving his arms nearly impossible. He was almost dragged down. Out of breath, he scrambled onto the sand bar and grabbed Chancey's bridle.

"Come on, boy. We'll get out of here. We'll be OK. You've got to swim to shore. I know it looks a long way, but you're strong. You can do it."

Chancey was circling the sand bar, pawing at the ground. Tom found it hard keeping Chancey still as he scrambled on top of him.

Tom patted his shoulder to settle him down. Then urging him forward, they plunged into the waves. When Chancey realized that he could swim, he wasn't so frightened. In spite of his words of encouragement, Tom didn't know if they could make it. Chancey was a courageous horse, but two hundred yards was a long way to swim.

They made good progress at first, but after five minutes, Chancey was beginning to struggle. The current was stronger than Tom had anticipated and he felt exhausted as he clung on, gripping until his legs were numb. Were they nearly halfway now? Tom didn't know. Surely they must be. But the shore didn't seem to be any closer. Bravely, they battled forward. Chancey snorted and spluttered as the water swirled, until slowly, the shore grew larger. They were getting closer. Tom started to feel more positive. Surely they could make it now. He thought he heard voices carrying in the sea air. They were almost there.

And suddenly they must have hit the sand. Chancey's nostrils were a fiery red as he forced his way through the crashing waves. He seemed to be walking along the sea-bed. They were at the foot of the cliffs. Tom felt shivery as they reached the path. He slid to the ground, unable to hold on any longer and everything went black...

Chapter 14

Chancey Forever!

Nick tensed with horror when Feather clattered into the yard, her reins dangling broken by her sides, her coat dank with sea water. She had come from the beach. Someone was in danger. He looked at his watch. Then at the tide sheet. Someone was in serious danger. Now.

Nick hurried over to Whispering Silver basking lazily in the sun and climbed into the saddle. Turning out of the yard, he called to Sarah to bring the Land Rover round the old coastal track to the top of the cliffs. No time to answer any questions.

He headed straight for the cliffs, the same route Tom had taken only half an hour earlier... through the fields and woods, to the open stretches beyond.

Nick reached the cliff path just as Georgina was scrambling her way up the blowhole. He gazed anxiously out to sea, willing himself to see something... anything. But there was nothing. Or was there? And then he saw – the outline of a horse on a sand bar. He looked harder. Chancey? Yes, but where was his rider? Now he could see a tiny speck moving halfway between the cliffs and the sand bar. Nick strained further forward. The speck seemed to be getting closer to the sand. It was a person. And then he saw someone else on the far side of the cliffs.

Georgina.

"What's happened?" he bellowed. "Who's that on the sand bar?"

"Ch...Ch...Chancey," Georgina stuttered.

"I can see that," Nick shouted. "But who's out there with him?"

"Tom."

"*Tom.*" Nick was flabbergasted. "What's he doing out there?"

"It's... it's my fault," Georgina spluttered, shivering now from both cold and fear. "I got caught and he wanted to go back for the horse. They will be all right, won't they? They'll be OK?"

"We'll soon see," Nick said grimly, scrambling down the path to the beach where the waves were crashing fiercely against the rocks.

It was a long way to swim. Nick had never felt so powerless. All he could do was watch. The pair seemed to be progressing slowly. And then he heard the noise of a car and Sarah appeared at the top of the cliffs. As she hurried down the path to join Nick, she needed no explanation. Training her eyes on the moving figures, she held her breath. The current was so strong but they were about halfway now. Could they make the shore?

"Clever boy," Sarah was saying. "He's following an angled route to take account of the currents."

Nick's mind was whirling. He couldn't watch. He

couldn't stop watching. He couldn't think straight. He didn't know what to do. Turning from the sea, he was aware that Sarah was giving him a running commentary. And he couldn't stop himself from thinking back over the years to the day he had first met Tom. He *had* to make it.

"Only fifty yards or so to go," said Sarah.

Nick snapped out of his trance as he realized he hadn't heard a word Sarah had been saying. He rushed forward as Chancey clawed at the rocks and stumbled up the path. Tom collapsed at his feet.

When Tom awoke, he was back in his bedroom at home. The curtains were drawn, but as his eyes became accustomed to the dark, he could just make out the shape of the large china horse on his book shelf. His head felt fuzzy. Had he had a bad dream?

His heart started to beat faster as, slowly, it all came back to him. "Mum, Mum, where are you?" He was panicking now.

Mrs. Buchanan rushed into the room.

"Why am I in bed?" he cried. "Where's Chancey? Did it all really happen?"

"Calm down," his mother said. "One question at a time. Everything's OK. You're just exhausted. Yes, it all happened, but you hit your head when you fell."

"But Georgina," said Tom.

"She's fine," said his mother. "In disgrace, but fine. She managed to climb up the blowhole. And Chancey's all right too. Showing off, but still in one piece. You've slept through the night, so you haven't missed out on anything."

"Oh," said Tom, a wave of relief overwhelming him. "I shouldn't have saved Georgina, should I?" he joked. "Then I'd have had Chancey all to myself."

"You were extremely brave," said his mother. "A lot has happened since then. You might find you have a few surprises," she added, drawing back the curtains. "Look outside."

Tom's head ached as he leaned out of his bed and stared out of the window. Then he laughed, for there was Chancey, walking on Mrs. Buchanan's tidy flowerbed. Alex was holding onto his head collar, waving up at Tom.

"What's going on?" he asked, stifling a giggle as Chancey pawed at his mother's prizewinning roses.

"I think your visitor will explain," she said mysteriously, as the door opened and Georgina came in, blushing.

"I'll leave you to talk," said Mrs. Buchanan, smiling encouragingly at Georgina as she left.

Nervously, Georgina came forwards.

"Why are you here?" he asked, bemused.

"Please listen, Tom," pleaded Georgina. "I-I know what I did was crazy," she stammered. "I thought I knew best."

Tom felt he was dreaming again. Was his cousin Georgina really standing in front of him, admitting she'd been wrong?

"I wanted to say thank you," Georgina went on. "You saved my life... I'm sorry for being so horrible. And I want you to have him."

"Who?"

"Chancey."

"Chancey?" Tom spluttered. It was the last thing he'd expected. "You mean you're giving him to me? Are you serious?"

"Totally." Georgina smiled. "I don't want to ride any more. I only took it up because I thought Dad wanted me to. Now he says he'd have been just as happy for me to do ballet. So, if you want him..." She hesitated, waiting for Tom to answer her. "We'd like him to go to a good home."

"Want him... *Want him*?" said Tom, more excited by the minute. "I can't believe it. Things like this don't happen. Tell me I'm not dreaming."

As if in response, there was a loud whinny from the garden. It was as though Chancey was trying to tell Tom it was really true. He was Tom's horse forever now, he seemed to be saying, not just for the summer.

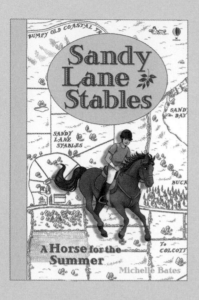

Sandy Lane Stables

A Horse for the Summer

Michelle Bates

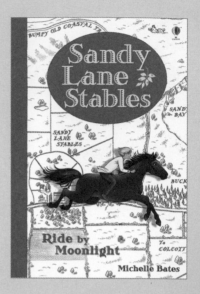

Sandy Lane Stables

Ride by Moonlight

Michelle Bates

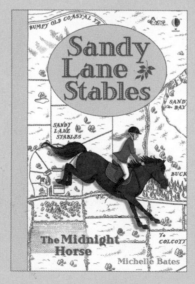

Sandy Lane Stables

The Midnight Horse

Michelle Bates